The Amazing Adventures of
Teddy Tum Tum

First published in Great Britain by
Michael O'Mara Books Limited
9 Lion Yard
Tremadoc Road
London SW4 7NQ

A CIP catalogue record for this book is
available from the British Library

ISBN 1-85479-027-7 (hardcover)
ISBN 1-85479-097-8 (paperback)

Editor: Anne Forsyth
Design: Marnie Searchwell

Typeset by Florencetype Ltd, Kewstoke, Avon
Printed and bound in Belgium by Proost International Book Production

The Amazing Adventures of
Teddy Tum Tum

Illustrated by Patrick Lowry
Written by Gillian Breese and Tony Langham

Michael O'Mara Books Limited

It was just after bedtime in the playroom. All the toys were sitting around, listening to the rain pitter-patter on the window pane. Teddy Tum Tum didn't like rain because it meant staying indoors. He wanted to be outside having one of his adventures.

"Never mind," said Rose-Anne The Rag Doll. "Why don't you tell us about one of your adventures instead?"

"Brilliant idea!" said Putney. "Tell them about the time we were captured by the Bongo Bongo Tribe."

"Oh, all right," agreed Teddy Tum Tum.

The toys gathered round to listen.

"It was a very dangerous mission," Tum Tum told them. "We had to plan very carefully for the perilous journey we were about to make."

"Where were you going?" asked one of the toys, beginning to feel frightened already.

"Into the unknown, up the great River Rambardo, where no bear had been before. It was full of wild animals, with huge eyes.

"I couldn't go alone. It was too dangerous. So I took my trusty friend Putney to carry supplies."

"Did you take a map?" enquired another toy.

"Adventurers don't use maps," scoffed Tum Tum. "We used our eyes and our ears and set sail into the unknown."

"There was danger everywhere. Great slimy creatures with rocks on their backs, huge hairy eight-legged beasts, watching and waiting, waiting and watching. Would they pounce, would they attack? We had no way of knowing. But there was no turning back. We paddled on deeper and deeper into the unknown and then disaster struck."

Rose-Anne gasped.

"The Great River Rambardo flowed faster and faster. The water swirled about us, waves crashed on to the deck. We tried to steer the boat through the raging torrent. She began to fill with water. We tried to bail her out but it was no use.

"All our supplies were hurled into the muddy water. Poor Putney was thrown overboard. I just managed to grab his ear as he floated past me. Then the boat slowly started to sink. We scrambled to the bank, exhausted and collapsed, glad that we were still alive."

"Our boat was wrecked.
Our supplies were lost.
Our stuffing was all wet.
But Putney and I didn't
give up. We rested a while
and discussed what to do.
There was only one thing
to do – to continue
on foot."

12

"We set off into the jungle not knowing what danger lay in store."

"Were you frightened?" asked Sammy the soldier.

"Not really," answered Tum Tum. "I'd been in situations more dangerous than this before."

"Go on," begged Sammy. "Please!"

"I led the way and Putney followed close behind. Every step led us further into danger. It was now getting darker and shadows loomed up menacingly in front of us but we crept cautiously forward, a step at a time, looking and listening, listening and looking."

"Putney thought he saw things."

"What things?" asked Eric the Elephant, not really wanting to know the answer.

"It's difficult to say, really. Just things."

Rose-Anne was hiding her face, hardly daring to listen.

"We could feel eyes watching us, following us. We couldn't see them but we knew they were there. We plodded on and on, then we saw it."

"We came face to face with the beast. It was huge. It was horrible. It sat there gazing down at us with its blazing yellow eyes."

"What did you do?" gasped Eric.

"Under the circumstances and all things considered, I gave the order to retreat."

"What does that mean?" asked Rose-Anne.

"Turn and run," said Putney.

"Retreat means retreat!" huffed Tum Tum. "Now, may I continue?"

"We ran through the undergrowth. Sharp thorns clawed at our fur. Suddenly I was stopped dead in my tracks, as I felt a sharp pain in my ear. It had caught on a long spiky thorn and I was stuck. As I tried to free myself, I could hear the beast fast approaching.

"I pulled with all my might, ripping my ear free just in time. We ran and ran until we could run no more. We dared to stop a moment to see if the beast was still following us. We turned round and saw only the shaking bushes where we had forced our way through."

"We wandered about this strange land for many days until we came upon a clearing in the jungle. In the middle of the clearing stood a tall stone, with a huge clock hand on top.

"What could it be? It was so tall that the clock hand cast a great shadow over us."

"As we explored the clearing we found some puzzling objects, including a long spear with twelve sharp prongs and a war chariot with only one wheel.

"Suddenly I felt myself falling. Putney tried to save me, but it was no use. I'd fallen into a bear pit!

"In a matter of seconds we were surrounded by the fiercest hunters in the land, the Bongo Bongo Tribe from Argar Don."

"Someone grabbed me and threw me into the war chariot. Poor Putney was dumped beside me and then we began to move. Where were we going and why?

"We seemed to go round and round but at last the chariot came to a halt. Was this the end? Would we ever see our friends again?

"We were in the clearing by the stone tower. We were lifted out and put right on top of it.

"I told Putney to be brave and prepare for the worst. There was a blood-curdling cry from one of the Tribe and then they all started to dance around us, whooping and yelling.

"The dance ended as suddenly as it began. The Bongo Bongo Tribe were strangely silent and still. Then they slowly walked towards us. We closed our eyes."

"Go on, go on," pleaded Rose-Anne.

"Well, in fact, they didn't want to harm us at all. On the contrary they wanted to be our friends. And guess what they did?"

"Do tell us," begged Rose-Anne.

"They made us Chiefs of their Tribe. They crowned us with golden crowns, studded with fabulous jewels."

"How exciting!" exclaimed Eric.

"Yes, it was quite exciting, but just one of the adventures I've had."

"Really?" said Rose-Anne, her eyes wide with wonder. "Please tell us more."

Teddy Tum Tum smiled to himself.
"Another time," he promised.
"Look, I think it's stopped raining."